THE HORROR OF HIGH RIDGE

BY JULIUS GOODMAN

ILLUSTRATED BY PAUL GRANGER

An R.A. Montgomery Book

BANTAM BOOKS
TORONTO · NEW YORK · LONDON · SYDNEY · AUCKLAND

RL 4, IL age 10 and up

THE HORROR OF HIGH RIDGE

A Bantam Book / December 1983

CHOOSE YOUR OWN ADVENTURE® is a registered trademark of
Bantam Books, Inc. Registered in U.S. Patent and Trademark
Office and elsewhere.

Original conception of Edward Packard

ISBN 0-553-23867-1

Published simultaneously in the United States and Canada

Bantam Books are published by Bantam Books, Inc. Its trademark, consisting of the word "Bantam Books" and the por-
trayal of a rooster, is Registered in U.S. Patent and Trademark
Office and in other countries. Marca Registrada. Bantam
Books, Inc., 666 Fifth Avenue, New York, New York 10103.

PRINTED IN THE UNITED STATES OF AMERICA

O   0 9 8 7 6 5 4 3

**To Kate
and to Ray**

WARNING!!!

Do not read this book straight through from beginning to end! These pages contain many different adventures you can have in the little town of High Ridge. From time to time as you read along, you will be asked to make a choice. Your choice may lead to success or disaster.

The adventures you take are a result of your choices. *You* are responsible because *you* choose! After you make a choice, follow the instructions to see what happens to you next.

Think carefully before you make a move. In this ghostly battle for revenge, any choice might be your last. Will you save yourself from the horror of High Ridge, or will you be trapped forever? It all depends on you.

Good luck!

You are standing at the window of your cabin, looking out onto the street. The waning moon shines quietly over High Ridge. It reflects on the frost beginning to form, giving each building of the small mountain town a glowing outline.

Earlier that evening, you said goodnight to your friends, Ricardo and Lisa, who have been spending the summer with you, searching for your great-uncle Rush's buried fortune. Then you settled down into your favorite parlor chair with an obscure volume of High Ridge history. You hoped this book would give you some clues to the whereabouts of the fortune. After a few hours you dozed off.

Then a sound outside startled you awake. You jumped to the window to look out. At first, you heard nothing.

You're beginning to wonder if you imagined it. Then the sound that woke you—a moaning scarier than any sound you have ever heard—begins again.

Turn to page 2.

"I don't like this," you say to yourself, thinking of the history of High Ridge. You've just read that a hundred years ago, and again fifty years ago, something happened in High Ridge so horrible that most people won't talk about it, and the accounts of those who do are very different. The links between both incidents are horrible moans and the disappearances or ghastly deaths of town residents.

You hop back into your chair and pull the blanket over your head.

Just as your pounding heart slows to normal, you are startled by a nearby scream.

You whip off the blanket. It's Lisa! The screaming stops. Lisa laughs with relief. "Oh, it's you. With the blanket over your head I thought you were a ghost. I woke up when I heard a noise. . . ." She points to your book, where it landed on the floor when you jumped up.

Ricardo comes running in. "What's going on? I heard screaming."

Go on to the next page.

Then the moaning starts again. Lisa and Ricardo run to the window. "What's that?" they shout together.

"I heard it a minute ago. I don't know what it is, but I don't like it."

"Let's go find out what it is," suggests Ricardo.

"Are you crazy?" cries Lisa. "Listen to it. It's scary."

"Well, sure it is. That's what makes it fun. I say let's leave the cabin and see what it is."

"Not me," says Lisa. "I don't want to go tramping around in the dark looking for whatever is making that horrible sound."

Both of them turn to look at you.

"Hold it, you two. Before we make a decision I have to tell you what I've been reading."

"Reading?" Lisa asks.

"Yeah, what is this, a book report?" Ricardo asks.

"No, wait," you say, a little angrily, "this is important. I've been reading this book, *High Ridge: An Oral History.* It's mostly a lot of ghost stories told by old-timers. Some of the ghosts are Indians; some are prospectors—they founded this town, remember."

"So what?"

"Quiet, Ricardo," Lisa says. "Go on, I want to hear more."

Go on to the next page.

"The stories about what happens with the ghosts are conflicting. Some say the prospector ghosts kill the Indian ghosts; in some it's the other way around; and in some, both kinds of ghosts kill—actually kill—townspeople."

"But that's all hooey," Ricardo says. "Even if you believe in ghosts, what does it have to do with us?"

"All the stories have one thing in common," you answer. "They all talk about horrible moans, just like the ones we're hearing." Just then, as if on cue, a moan drifts into the cabin.

Everyone is silent for a moment. Then Ricardo says, "Well, I'm ready to go look around, if you are." He doesn't sound quite as certain as he did before. Lisa, though, sounds surer than before. "Not me," she says curtly.

If you decide you'd rather stay in the cabin and try to ignore whatever is moaning outside, turn to page 6.

If you decide to investigate the eerie sounds, go on to the next page.

"Let's go," you announce. "I really don't think there's anything *too* awful out there."

"You're *kidding,*" says Lisa.

"C'mon, Lisa, you don't believe in ghosts and spooks and stuff like that, do you? It's probably just some kid practicing for Halloween, or a rusty gate swinging in the wind."

"A rusty gate?" Lisa is really upset now. "And, yes, I do believe in ghosts. At least, I don't *dis*believe in them. I am not going out there." Lisa crosses her arms and turns away.

"Ricardo, don't just sit there. Help me talk some sense into Lisa."

"There's no wind," Ricardo says gravely.

"Huh?"

"I said there's no wind."

"What does that have to do with anything?"

"That means it can't be a creaky gate."

"Hah!" Lisa faces you again. "I told you so."

"Ricardo, that's not much help." You stop in consternation; you don't know what to do. Everybody is silent for a few minutes. Finally, you have an idea. But before you can say anything, you smell kerosene. Then the room plunges into darkness.

Turn to page 9.

6

"I'm staying in the cabin," you say. Lisa lets out a sigh of relief. The moaning starts again. You can't tell whether it is louder or closer.

Ricardo looks out the window. "Well, I'm not going out there by myself, that's for sure. You're a couple of chickens." You know he doesn't really mean it. Besides, he looks relieved.

"Let's go to bed," you say, bending to pick up your book. Just as you touch it, you hear the front window crash. An arrow flies over your head and into the wall.

"Duck!" Ricardo yells as everybody drops to the floor.

You turn to look at the arrow, which is hard to see in the dim light of the kerosene lamp. Then you realize the arrow is disappearing!

"What the . . ." you start to say, but Ricardo interrupts you.

"Let's get out of here," he says urgently. Lisa nods; she looks too scared to talk.

"I don't know if it's safer outside or in," you say, staring at the spot where the arrow was.

If you decide it's safer to stay in the cabin, turn to page 12.

If you decide you'd rather try to make it to your jeep and leave town as quickly as possible, turn to page 8

"Let's get to the jeep," you finally decide.

"I'll have to pack," Lisa says.

"Pack? Are you crazy?" responds Ricardo.

"Ricardo's right. The faster we get out of here, the better. Let's go right now. No, Ricardo, leave the lamp lit. Whoever is out there will think—I hope—that we're still here."

All of you grab warm sweaters and slip outside. The mountain air is cold at night, even in summer. You climb quietly into the jeep, which is fortunately parked on an incline. You leave the headlights off, release the handbrake, and coast silently downhill. The moon casts enough light to drive by.

Your cabin is on the edge of town, and it's easy to coast down to the main road leading out of the mountains. As you turn onto the road, you let out a sigh. "Whew, I'm glad we're out of there."

"Indians! I saw Indians! Back there!" cries Ricardo.

"Aw, c'mon, Ricardo. You're just hallucinating," Lisa says.

"No, really! I swear it!"

"The moonlight in the mountains plays tricks on the eyes," you say. "Lisa's probably right. Besides, you're just thinking about the arrow and that got you to thinking about Indians. . . ."

"See what I mean?" says Ricardo.

"WATCH OUT!"

Turn to page 10.

"Don't panic, anybody. It's only the lamp. It just ran out of kerosene."

"Why don't you get electricity like everyone else?" Lisa sounds really angry. Ricardo is chuckling to himself.

"I told you!" you reply angrily. "I like the old-time feel of the cabin the way it is. It's just like when it was my great-uncle's. It wouldn't be the same with electricity."

Except for the darkness in the cabin, everything is as it was before. You have forgotten what you were going to say. Then out of the blackness comes the moaning sound. Your chest feels cold. You hear another noise mixed in with the moans.

"Do you hear that?" you whisper.

"Wh-what? The m-m-moans?" Lisa asks.

"Sh!" says Ricardo. "Yes, I hear it too. Cries for help."

"I hear it now!" Lisa says after a pause. "Let's go!"

Turn to page 11.

10

You jam on the brakes. Lisa's warning came just in time. The road has disappeared under a rock slide. You come to a stop inches from a large boulder. Everybody gets out.

"We can't drive any farther with the road blocked," Lisa says. "I guess we start walking."

"Unless we camp here," Ricardo adds.

Both suggestions sound sensible to you, but you're also wondering if your imagination has gone wild. Maybe you should consider turning around and heading back to town.

If you decide to leave the jeep and start walking down the road, turn to page 29.

If you decide to camp here, turn to page 22.

If you decide to turn around and head back to town, turn to page 13.

You all run to your rooms and hastily dress in warm clothes. The night air is cold in the mountains. As you race out the door, you suddenly realize you don't know where you're going or what you're doing.

"Wait a minute!" you say. "What are we doing?"

"We're going to help whoever is calling for help, of course," responds Lisa.

"What about the ghosts?" you ask. "Remember the stories."

"Aw, they're just stories," Ricardo says. "But maybe we should climb the church tower first and look the town over."

"I wonder if maybe we shouldn't go over to Mr. Phillip's house first?"

"Who's he?" Lisa asks.

"The unofficial town historian. He's lived here all his life and knows everything about High Ridge. He's also our nearest neighbor."

If you decide to respond to the cries for help, turn to page 21.

If you decide to climb to the church tower, turn to page 16.

If you decide to head over to Mr. Phillip's house, turn to page 27.

"Let's stay put," you say. "I don't think I want to be roaming around outside—at least not right now. Everybody keep down and crawl over to the corner, away from the windows."

When everybody is safely out of range, you again look at the spot where the arrow hit the wall. Only a small, ragged scar in the wood remains.

"I'd say from the spot on the wall and the broken window that even disappearing arrows can kill."

Lisa shudders. "Ricardo, don't say stuff like that!"

As if answering Lisa, the moaning begins again. You crawl over to the kerosene lamp and blow it out.

"Why'd you do that?" Lisa asks.

"I think we're safer from more arrows if the room's not lit," you answer.

"Don't forget bullets," Ricardo adds.

"What do you mean?"

"Remember what you read. Not only Indian ghosts are shooting arrows out there—we probably have to worry about prospector ghosts shooting guns, too. I wonder what this is all about."

Turn to page 14.

Maybe your imagination has gone wild. "Don't you guys think we're getting a little carried away here?" you say.

"What do you mean?" Ricardo asks.

"I mean maybe we should go back to town."

"That's crazy," Lisa says.

"Is it?" you respond. "We all saw the arrow— or think we did. Then we panicked. What I mean is, there's probably a perfectly rational explanation for the whole thing. Maybe someone's playing a trick on us. Some little kid probably fell down from laughing so hard when we took off in the jeep. Besides, the more I think about walking down the road in the dark or staying here, the less I like it."

Turn to page 24.

14

"Me, too," you say. "I'm going to peek out the window.

"Don't!" warns Lisa.

"It's okay, with the lamp out," you say, crawling to the window. Carefully you peer out over the sill.

The empty street is bright in the moonlight. Nothing seems wrong, but then you notice a reddish glow in the sky behind the Shaws' house. You crawl back to the corner.

"What's up?" Ricardo and Lisa ask in unison.

"Can't see much at all, except what might be a fire over toward the center of town. I want to check it out."

"I'll come," offers Ricardo.

"Not me," says Lisa. "I'd rather stay here."

"No, you wouldn't. Not after we leave."

"Yes, I would. Go ahead without me. I'll be all right alone."

If you decide to leave Lisa while you and Ricardo check outside, turn to page 20.

If you try to convince Lisa to come with you, turn to page 17.

You lead the way to the church tower. The night air is cold on your face. You are warm, but you find yourself shivering nonetheless.

The moans occur only once as you walk to the tower. They are hollow sounding, not terribly loud, and you are unable to locate their source: the sound surrounds you. When the moans stop, you look at each other as if to say: *What are we doing here?*

You continue on, however, and soon reach the tower.

The church is open. You climb the stairs hurriedly to the top.

"There's nothing to see!" Lisa wails, frustrated.

"Keep looking on that side, Lisa," says Ricardo. "There must be something."

You all keep looking, but nothing appears. The red glow is not a fire; it's just a red glow over a small park on the north end of town. Except for the glow everything seems normal—until you hear footsteps coming up the tower stairs.

The tread is slow, but steady. It does not sound human.

You realize with a start that the stairs are the only way out of the tower—except jumping.

Turn to page 35.

"C'mon, Lisa. You know you don't want to be left alone."

"I know I don't want to go out there!"

"But when we're gone, you'll be sitting here, in the dark, alone, nobody around to . . ."

"Oh, stop it, Ricardo! Okay, I'll come with you. But if I die, I'll never speak to you again!"

You stare at each other in the moonlight coming in through the windows. Then you all burst into laughter.

The laughter makes you feel good again. You wish that whatever is going on outside would stop.

Silently you all sneak out the back door and creep away from the house.

"Where are we going?" whispers Ricardo.

"Over to the Hubbard place. We can watch the street from there without being seen."

The Hubbard place is an abandoned, weathered, two-story house you've explored before. Warning Ricardo and Lisa to avoid the creaky fourth step, you quietly climb the stairs to the second-floor balcony. You position yourselves behind the railing, which has cut-outs in it. Nothing moves on the street. The red glow flickers in the sky.

Go on to the next page.

18

Lisa nudges you and points to a spot near your house. Something's moving.

You hold your breath, afraid to move. Ricardo and Lisa are still as statues. Then you see that it's an Indian!

Flickering in the moonlight, he silently creeps out into the street. He looks up and down the street as if he's watching for something, then heads for your house. You wonder if he's the one who shot the vanishing arrow.

Just as he is peering stealthily into your front window, he is stabbed in the back by a tall old-time prospector.

You glance at Ricardo and Lisa. They look as scared as you feel. When you look back to the street, you are surprised to see the collapsed Indian get up! Drawing a tomahawk from his belt, he buries it in the prospector's chest. Then the two of them vanish into thin air!

Turn to page 25.

"Lisa, you *sure* you want to be left alone?"

"Yes." Lisa answers shortly. You're not too sure she means it, but you have to take her word for it.

You and Ricardo step out the back door. You peer around the corner. The street is still empty, and there is still a red glow in the sky.

"Shall we check out that glow?" asks Ricardo.

You are about to say yes when the moaning starts again, louder and clearer now that you are outside. It seems to come from one end of the tower, and sounds like someone in agony.

"Maybe we should see what the noise is." Ricardo says in a strained voice, gripping your shoulder.

If you decide to keep to your original plan and investigate the red glow, turn to page 26.

If you decide to check out the moaning instead, turn to page 36.

"We have to go to whoever's calling for help," you say finally.

"Good," Lisa responds.

"Yeah, I guess. I mean, if *I* were calling for help, I'd hope somebody would come."

"Me, too," Ricardo says. "Let's get some warm clothes and get going."

Just as you are ready to leave, you hear a knock on the front door. Without thinking, you open it. In walks an old Indian.

"Good evening," he says. "I am Chief Walking Eagle. I have been dead for a hundred years. I need your help."

Turn to page 28.

You decide to camp for the night.

You find a relatively soft patch of gravel and, grabbing the blankets from the back of the jeep, the three of you huddle together for a long wait.

Toward morning somebody does come up the road, but you are in no condition to greet him. Along with twelve other High Ridge townspeople, you three are rushed to the hospital.

Go on to the next page.

That afternoon, the headlines in the local newspaper read:

HORROR AT HIGH RIDGE

High Ridge, Calif. (AP) Something has frightened fifteen residents of this small mining town in the Sierra Nevada right into the intensive care unit of the University Medical Center in Sacramento. The same mystery force killed ten others and scared the thirty remaining inhabitants into leaving town.

"I don't know what it is," said Lottie Howard, one longtime resident, "and I don't care to stay and find out. If you could see the faces on those people, you wouldn't want to stick around either."

Hospital spokesmen will only say that the fifteen people are "stable and under observation," but one hospital employee said unofficially: "If they were dead, you'd say they were scared to death because that's how they look, but they're not dead—they're in comas. I don't know what you'd call it."

Police have cordoned off the town, and refuse to comment further at this time.

The End

Ricardo and Lisa are both hesitant about returning to town, but finally they decide to go with you.

You turn the jeep around and head back to town. Lisa tells a lot of terrible jokes; Ricardo is quiet. Suddenly he yells, "Stop!"

"What's the matter?" you shout, slamming on the brakes.

"The place where I saw those Indians—or whatever they were—is just around the corner. I think we should check it out on foot before driving through there."

If you decide to follow Ricardo's suggestion, turn to page 42.

If you decide Ricardo is just nervous and you should drive on, turn to page 44.

"Did you see that?"

"Yes," Ricardo and Lisa reply together.

"Wh-what do you think it was?" asks Lisa.

"Well, it's not anybody ordinary—I think."

"Brilliant, Ricardo," Lisa answers sarcastically.

"Cut it out!" you say. "We've got enough trouble without you two bickering."

"What do we do now?"

"I'm sure that pair isn't alone. We should either split, or stay in town and hide. I don't think I want to meet either of those guys or their friends."

"Would it be safe to take the jeep?" Lisa asks.

"Sure, why not?" replies Ricardo.

"It doesn't feel right," you answer. "I think we should either hide somewhere in town or get out of here on foot."

If you decide to leave town, turn to page 45.

If you decide to find a hiding place, turn to page 59.

"Let's check out the glow," you tell Ricardo. "If it's a fire, we have to get help."

Ricardo follows you down the eerie street. You stay near the houses, moving from shadow to shadow.

You try to figure out what makes the street feel so oppressive and ominous tonight. Only the moaning and the red glow are unusual. It might be—who knows?—just a creaky gate and some colored outdoor floodlights.

A hand grabs your shoulder and pulls you roughly into a dark, narrow alley.

Turn to page 51.

"Let's go over to Mr. Phillip's house," you announce.

"What about the cries for help?"

"I don't know, Lisa. I don't like any of our alternatives—including staying in the cabin. But the cries for help are coming from that way anyway. I think it would be good to stop in at Mr. Phillip's house." You pause, then say, "Maybe he's the one calling for help."

"Okay—I guess." With Lisa's tentative approval, you set off.

Although it is not far to your destination, it seems to take forever. It is as if the whole town is holding its breath and watching you walk down the street.

As you approach the house, caution slows you down even further. Finally the house appears. Suddenly you stop dead in your tracks.

"Wait! Did you see that?"

"Yes."

"What do we do?"

"Watch him," Ricardo says as he drops to the ground and crawls forward. You don't want to be left behind so you follow, Lisa bringing up the rear.

Turn to page 32.

"Dead for a hundred years?" Ricardo exclaims.

"Yes. Please sit down, my friends. I will explain. I will answer your questions when I am done.

"When prospectors founded this town a hundred years ago, they made peace with the local Indians and left them a plot of land near the new town. It was a sacred site for my people.

"One night the prospectors, celebrating a gold strike, were drinking heavily. That night was a ceremonial event for my tribe, who sang as they marched to the sacred site with their ceremonial objects. The prospectors descended on the Indians and massacred them. The next day they mined the site, taking the gold they found and burying all else under rock piles. When the rest of the tribe retaliated, they were also wiped out. What happened later I do not understand, but now three times it has come to pass that those who were killed were compelled to return to kill one another over and over again, from midnight until dawn. Even worse, they also kill the people who live in the town.

"It will stop when someone, perhaps you, removes one of the ceremonial objects buried at the sacred site and parades it through town. The spirits will follow it back to the sacred site, where I will perform a special ceremony.

"This and only this will stop the horror in High Ridge."

Turn to page 30.

"I don't know about you guys, but I'd rather walk. This place feels awful spooky."

You grab a flashlight and the blankets from the back of the jeep and leave with Ricardo and Lisa.

As you climb over the rock slide, you glance back down the road. You can see farther up the mountain where you know the town is. You wonder what that dim red glow in the sky is. Then you clamber down the other side of the rock pile.

Walking is difficult. The cliff on your right blocks the moon from lighting the road. Every few minutes one of you stumbles on a rock or into a hole, but you decide you can't use the flashlight just for walking. It wouldn't hold out all night anyway.

About two miles down the road, you round a sharp bend. A pair of headlights shines in your face. A voice shouts from the dark, "Stop! Hands up and don't move!"

Turn to page 48.

As the chief finishes his speech, his appearance alters slightly. At first you aren't sure what is different; then you notice he's disappearing!

You, Ricardo, and Lisa are speechless. You know that they are thinking the same thing you are: Will you obey the chief's request?

If you decide to help the chief, turn to page 40.

If you decide that helping the chief is too scary, turn to page 52.

An Indian moves silently around the house, peeking in the windows. As you are wondering how to get warning to Mr. Phillip without giving yourself away, the Indian steps back suddenly and shoots an arrow through the side window.

Then he disappears into the air as if he had never existed. Before you can stop her, Lisa runs to the house and flings open the door. The silence is broken by her screams.

You rush to the house. Lisa stands by the door, hands over her eyes. Mr. Phillip is sprawled on the floor, an arrow in his chest. His terror-stricken eyes are wide open. He is dead.

Turn to page 34.

You freeze, unable to move. As you stare at Mr. Phillip's body, you notice that the arrow is gradually disappearing until it is gone.

You turn to Ricardo and Lisa. They have been watching the arrow, too.

"Keep watching," says Ricardo. You wonder what he is talking about as you turn back to the corpse.

The body is disappearing! A minute later, it vanishes completely.

"N-now wh-what?" whispers Lisa.

If you decide to go back to your house and hide there, turn to page 71.

If you decide that you must have information on what is happening, turn to page 101.

If you decide it would be safer to stay where you are, turn to page 83.

"What do we do?"

"Keep calm, Lisa," whispers Ricardo.

"Keep calm! Are you kidding?"

"He's right," you say. "Lisa, there's nothing we *can* do." You sound braver than you feel. The footsteps are much closer now. "I guess we just face whoever it is."

"Or *what*-ever."

"Oh, Ricardo." Lisa is almost in tears.

Then the stair-climber comes into view. It's neither a prospector nor an Indian! It's just a young man.

Lisa plops down in relief. You and Ricardo let out a sigh. But then you notice that your visitor is a little unusual. For one thing, he's dressed in old-fashioned clothes; for another, he flickers, turning almost invisible at times.

Turn to page 37.

36

"Let's investigate that moaning," you tell Ricardo, and you head off to your right.

"Wait a minute," Ricardo says urgently. "Where are you going?"

"Toward the moaning," you answer, surprised. "Isn't that what we agreed on?"

"Yes, but the moaning came from over there." Ricardo points in the opposite direction.

You stare at him in amazement. "No, it came from up the street!"

You are about to ask Ricardo if this is a joke when the moaning starts again, only to stop a moment later. You both say to each other, "See, I told you. It's coming from over there."

If you decide to head in the direction you think the sound is coming from, turn to page 49.

If you decide to head in the direction Ricardo thinks the sound is coming from, turn to page 60.

"Who are you?" you ask.

"What I am is more appropriate," he answers.

"Wh-what?" stammers Ricardo.

"Don't be alarmed. I won't hurt you. I will try to help as I tried once before, but I don't suppose it will work now, either. I guess you'd like the whole story."

You're not sure you would, but there doesn't seem to be a choice.

"Shortly after this town was founded," the visitor begins, "some of the founding prospectors came upon a group of Indians who were engaged in a religious ceremony. The prospectors were drunk and were frightened by the Indians. They attacked and slaughtered them, desecrated their ritual objects, and ruined their sacred site. The rest of the Indian community retaliated later. Perhaps because the interrupted ceremony was a burial ritual, the victims of both sides became spirits that haunt this town.

"Twice since then, the last time about fifty years ago, all the spirits reappeared and, compelled by some horrible force, killed one another—over and over again. Over the spirits hangs a red glow. Whether the actions of the spirits cause the glow, or the glow directs the actions, I don't know."

Go on to the next page.

"But how do you fit in?" interrupts Ricardo.

"As horrible as this grotesque and involuntary game is, there is something more horrible yet.

"When the spirits return to town, they are also compelled to kill people there."

"How horrible!" Lisa exclaims.

"Is that what happened to you?" you ask.

"Yes," he replies. "The Indian chief appeared and asked me to help end the horror. I tried unsuccessfully."

"What were you supposed to do?" Ricardo asks.

"The chief will have to tell you. I can stay here no longer."

The last word drifts back to you as—before your terrified gaze—the speaker throws himself off the tower.

Turn to page 41.

"We *have* to help," Ricardo says.

"Yes," Lisa adds. "There's no way we can turn him down."

"Exactly what I was thinking," you say. "I suppose we ought to grab some shovels and head over to the sacred site he was talking about."

"Do you know where it is?"

"I think so. You know, it's strange. I've been there several times, just walking around, and I always felt uncomfortable. It's as though there's something evil there. I guess I know why now."

"Sounds like a wonderful place," Lisa says.

"We better go," Ricardo says.

You head out the door, you and Lisa with shovels over your shoulders, Ricardo carrying two flashlights.

Turn to page 43.

You all rush to the tower's edge. The spirit floats down, landing on his feet, and runs off— toward the red glow.

"That was terrible," says Lisa. "We *must* help. How awful to be caught in such a horror!"

"What if we fail, too?" asks Ricardo.

"But we won't," says Lisa. "We're special. And there are three of us."

Lisa's explanation isn't too convincing. You, too, would like to try to stop the horror, but you're also afraid of getting caught in it.

If you decide to help stop what is happening, turn to page 61.

If you think it is too dangerous, turn to page 53.

You might as well humor Ricardo.

"Okay, Ricardo, we'll stop here and take a look. How do you want to do it?"

"I thought we'd climb up the cliff and look around."

"Why not sneak along the side of the road?" Lisa suggests. "Nobody would see us, and in the moonlight we'd be able to spot anything on the cliff."

If you decide to climb the cliff, turn to page 64.

If you decide to creep along the road, turn to page 58.

The moaning continues, but now that you know what causes it, it doesn't bother you as much.

When you reach the site, Lisa turns to you. "I see what you mean. This place feels *awful.*"

"We'd better get to work," Ricardo says. "Any idea where to dig?"

"Nope."

"Might as well try here, then," he says.

You take turns digging and holding the flashlights, but you don't find anything. Hours later, just before dawn, you are tired, sore, and disappointed. Lisa calls for a break and a conference.

"I suppose we have to keep digging until we run out of time. I wonder if there's another way to do this."

"You heard the chief," Ricardo says.

"You know," you say after a pause, "I had a thought. Mrs. Grundy gave me the key to the library this morning. I wonder if we could find more clues there, now that we have some information."

If you decide to see what you can find at the library, turn to page 55.

If you think the chief told you all you need to know, keep digging, and turn to page 63.

"Ricardo, you're just too nervous," you say as you step on the gas. "You were just hallucinating after seeing that arrow. . . ."

"Wait!" Ricardo and Lisa shout, but it's too late. A rain of bullets hits down on you. In your last earthly glimpse, you discover Ricardo was wrong. It wasn't Indians with arrows on the cliff. It was prospectors with guns.

The End

"Let's get out of here," says Lisa.

"Exactly my idea," you answer.

"How do we do it?" asks Ricardo.

"There's a trail behind this house. It's not used much, and not well marked. I think we can sneak out of town without being seen."

"You *think*?"

"I *hope*. C'mon, let's go."

But before you can move, strong arms grab the three of you from behind. You cry out in pain and fright.

"Scream your heart out. It won't help," says one of your captors—an old prospector.

You are half dragged, half carried to the cemetery near the church.

Turn to page 47.

There you are tied to stakes in front of a smoldering fire. A dozen or so Indian braves are also tied up. Nearby stands a group of prospectors who seem to have just stepped out of a museum exhibit. They are oblivious to your pleas for mercy.

One of your captors stoops by the fire and picks up a long stick—no! It's a piece of steel, one end glowing fire-red. Slowly he advances, holding out the hot iron toward you.

The End

Suddenly you recognize the voice: it's the sheriff! He recognizes you at the same time.

"Kill the lights, Sam," he tells his deputy. "I know these folks." He turns to you. "Say, what are you doing out here, this time of night?"

You laugh. "I was just about to ask you the same question, Sheriff."

"We're investigating complaints of screams, rioting, and other disturbances up in High Ridge. You don't know anything about that, do you?"

You, Ricardo, and Lisa look at each other, and all start talking at once.

"Whoa. One at a time, please."

Quickly you describe the moanings, the broken window, the disappearing arrow, and the rock slide. The sheriff nods and makes little "mm-hm" sounds. "We're heading up to town now," he says. "I'd like to take your jeep to town. Okay?"

You think you'd like to go with him and see what's happening in town. You feel it would be safer to accompany the sheriff than to be alone.

If you decide to go to town with the sheriff, turn to page 79.

If you decide you'd rather keep heading away from town, turn to page 66.

"We'll go this way," you say as you head toward where you heard the sound. Ricardo follows.

The farther you go up the street, the worse you feel. It's as if the atmosphere is becoming heavier and heavier. You turn to talk to Ricardo, but you can't seem to speak. He acts as if nothing is the matter, and urges you forward without speaking.

You approach the end of the street. The road curves around the last building, then climbs higher into the mountains. There is a hill on the other side of the street that conceals a small park.

You feel irresistibly drawn to the park, as though a giant hand is pulling you.

Turn to page 67.

It's Ricardo!

"What are you doing? You scared me half to death," you say.

"Shh! Keep still. I was walking behind you, checking things out. Everything was copacetic." You can't help smiling. "Copacetic" is Ricardo's special word this month; he uses it whenever he can. "But suddenly, I felt this need to hide." He pauses, then violently whispers, "Shh! Stay back!"

You slip farther back into the shadowed alley, keeping an eye on the street. Then you hear faint footsteps. You see a flicker as someone walks past the alley. An Indian! He is followed by three others, all hard to see. Then follows a procession of what looks like old-time prospectors, tied together and moaning horribly. You look closer. Some of the prospectors have arrows protruding from their bodies. The others have tomahawks buried in their backs.

You glance in terror at Ricardo but cannot see him in the darkness. You look out onto the street. Another Indian files past, with a ghastly grin on his face. Slung over his shoulder is a decapitated head. He holds it by its long, dirty hair, while blood from its neck drips down his back.

A low moan escapes your lips as you faint and slump to the dirt of the alley.

The End

You decide you can't do what the chief asks. You tell Ricardo and Lisa your decision.

"What do we do, then?" Lisa asks.

"We either stay here in the cabin all night or leave in the jeep."

"Whew," Ricardo says. "Both sound dangerous. Which do you want to do?"

If you decide to leave town in the jeep, turn to page 54.

If you decide to stay in the cabin, turn to page 75.

"It sounds too dangerous to me," you announce. "I don't know about you two, but I'm sure there must be a way to stop this horror without getting involved."

"I'm not so sure," Ricardo answers. "Sometimes the only way to end something is to get right in the middle of it."

"But what if the middle of it is deadly?"

"Lisa's right, Ricardo. 'He who leaves, lives to fight again,' or something like that."

"Maybe, but I'm not positive. I think that . . . wait! What's that?"

You heard it, too. The wind has picked up. It too seems to be moaning.

You have been huddling together on the floor of the tower since your visitor left. Now you stand up. The red glow has spread; it's covering the whole sky now. You sink back to the floor. Ricardo and Lisa join you.

Again the moaning starts and grows louder and louder. The red glow seems to hang over the tower, but you're afraid to look.

The three of you spend the night on the tower floor, arms around one another. You can't decide which is worse: not knowing what is going on down there, or thinking about finding out.

The End

"Let's get out of here!" you yell, as you head toward the jeep.

Lisa and Ricardo sit stonily by your side as you drive down the road. You can tell they don't like your decision to leave. You don't like your decision to leave either, but you didn't have much of a choice—staying was just too dangerous.

You hope you don't regret your decision too much.

The End

You run to the library. You meet no ghosts on the way.

When you let yourself in the massive door, you are startled by Mrs. Grundy's voice. "Who's there?"

She is relieved to find out it's you, and starts to tell you about her terrifying night and her decision to hide in the library. Normally you would just listen to her quietly; she's a forceful woman used to dominating the conversation. To her surprise, you tell her *your* story.

"I'm not sure I believe a *word* of what you're saying," she says when you are finished, "but after what I saw tonight with my own eyes . . ." She drifts into silence for a minute, then says, "What about the mysterious statue of the Indian chief upstairs in the museum?"

"Of course!" you exclaim. You bound up the stairs, shouting, "I forgot all about it!"

Go on to the next page.

56

You recall that one day, about a hundred years ago, the statue of the Indian chief with the tomahawk mysteriously appeared at the library. There was a strange poem on a plaque around its neck. No one has ever figured out what the words mean. The statue was moved up to the museum, installed in a glass case, and practically forgotten.

You stop to read the poem preserved with the statue:

> *Swing me twice when the glow arrives,*
> *You'll save yourself and other lives.*
> *Swing me thrice as the horror goes,*
> *You'll bring peace between the foes.*

With shouts of "I've got it! I've got it!" you break the case, grab the tomahawk, and race downstairs and out the door.

As you run back to the sacred site to pick up Ricardo and Lisa, you wonder if there's enough time left.

Turn to page 76.

"Let's check it out from the side of the road,"
you say. "We may not see as much, but I think it
will be safer than climbing the cliff in the dark."

After a few whispered directions to Ricardo and
Lisa, you all creep along the path just below the
roadway.

The closer you get to your chosen lookout
point, the more prickly your skin feels. You sense
that someone is nearby and watching, yet when
you look around, you see no one.

Lisa puts her hand on your shoulder to stop
you. The touch almost gives you a heart attack. "I
feel as if somebody is spying on us," she whispers. Ricardo nods yes.

"Me too," you whisper back. "Maybe Ricardo's
right." You glance at him. Being right doesn't
appeal as much to him now as it usually does; he
looks scared. So does Lisa, and you realize you're
scared, too.

"Do you want to leave now?" Lisa quickly nods
yes. Ricardo hesitates, then shrugs, and says no.
You hesitate. You want to leave quickly, but
you're also curious to explore more.

*If you decide to continue to the lookout you've
chosen, turn to page 77.*

If you decide to leave, turn to page 65.

"I'm for hiding," you say. "I just don't know where."

"We could go back to the house," Ricardo offers.

"I can't think of any place else—wait, what about the library? I still have the key Mrs. Grundy, the librarian, gave me this morning. The trouble is we'd have to sneak over to the library without being seen."

"And the trouble with the house," adds Lisa, "is that we've already been attacked there once."

"So what do we do?" asks Ricardo desperately.

If you decide to try the library, turn to page 81.

If you decide to go back to the house, turn to page 70.

You shrug. "We'll go your way, Ricardo." He grins and sets off down the street.

You are almost at the end of the street when Ricardo turns to you. "Maybe you were right about the direction. We haven't heard or seen a thing this way."

"Maybe, but let's go to Cross Street and down a little farther. Sound bounces around in these mountain towns. You could still be right."

As you start to leave, you glimpse something in the alley next to you.

A ghostly figure flaps its arms slowly. It starts to moan horribly, and you are transfixed with terror.

Turn to page 72.

"I don't like it, but I *must* try to help stop the horror."

"I'm with you," Lisa says.

"Me, too," Ricardo chimes in.

"Well, great, you guys. Have any suggestions? I'm at a loss."

"I suppose we need the Indian chief."

"We can't just walk around looking for him."

"Wait!" you cry. "I just remembered something. In the museum that's upstairs in the library there's a statue of an Indian chief, with a poem that nobody's ever figured out. I can't remember it, but it might have something to do with this."

"It sounds weird, but possible," says Ricardo.

"Shall we go to the museum and read the poem?" you ask.

"Unless we try to find the real chief," Lisa says.

If you decide to go to the museum, turn to page 74.

If you decide to look for the chief, turn to page 86.

"Look, I'm sure the chief wants us to succeed. He wouldn't steer us wrong."

"You mean keep digging?" Lisa asks.

"Right," you respond.

"But I'm all blistered," Ricardo complains, "and my shoulders are killing me."

"Take a break, then. Go sit down for a little while. Take a walk around. . . ."

"But keep close," Lisa interrupts.

"Yeah, and keep your eyes peeled."

"Okay," Ricardo says as he hands over his shovel.

"You know," Lisa says, between shovelsful of dirt, "it's almost dawn.

"Yeah. The sky's getting lighter. I'm scared we're going to run out of time." You shovel faster.

Then Ricardo comes running up. "They're coming! They're coming! We've got to do something!"

"Who?" "What?" you and Lisa ask.

"The ghosts! They've banded together and are headed this way. They're after us! Hurry! We've got to get out of here."

Turn to page 87.

64

"Let's climb," you say. "There's a place over here that's easy to get up."

"I wish we had a gun," Lisa says as you hop out of the jeep. Her comment reminds you that you stuck your rifle in the back seat yesterday. It's only a .22, but it might scare somebody off.

As you reach for it, you pause. It's not really powerful. Perhaps it would cause more trouble than it's worth. On the other hand, maybe it's better than nothing.

If you decide to take the rifle, turn to page 93.

If you decide to forget about the .22, turn to page 114.

"Let's leave," you whisper. Ricardo lets out a sigh of relief. You can see his breath in the cold.

The three of you turn back. Ricardo is now in the lead. Before he takes a step, he peers up for a last look around. Instantly he stiffens. You can see his face getting whiter and whiter in the moonlight. His eyes bulge and his mouth drops open. Then he faints dead away.

Before you and Lisa can move, two hands reach down and grab you by your collars. You and Lisa are hauled up by strong arms to face whatever it was Ricardo saw.

The End

"No problem, Sheriff, take my jeep." The sheriff calls out his thanks and roars away. You, Ricardo, and Lisa continue trudging down the mountain.

Finally you reach the highway and catch a ride into Barton City. Later that day you read a newspaper account of the horror that visited High Ridge. You are shocked to learn of the deaths of ten townspeople and of the disappearance of the sheriff and his deputy.

You wonder just what's going on in High Ridge, but you don't feel like going back to find out.

The End

From the top of the hill you look down into the park. Ricardo stands next to you.

Down among the cottonwoods a scene unfolds that is hard for you to watch. A group of ragged Indians, wielding bows and tomahawks, chase an equally ragged bunch of prospectors. They seem to flicker in the moonlight as they run counterclockwise around the park. Occasionally one of the prospectors breaks away and is felled by either an Indian's knife or an arrow. As he falls dying to the ground, he moans—the horrible moans you heard before.

But the scene becomes yet stranger and uglier. In time the dead prospector gets up and runs to his group. You watch him get killed again—as horribly as before—while he runs around the park.

Then, to your amazement, everybody runs in the reverse direction. Only this time the prospectors pursue and kill the Indians!

Go on to the next page.

While you watch this scene, an Indian breaks away and—chased by a knife-wielding prospector—runs directly toward you. You are paralyzed by fear. The prospector catches up to the Indian just two yards from you and sinks the knife into his back. The Indian falls, moaning loudly. His blood sprays in an arc, drenching you and Ricardo.

It burns like fire! You scream in pain. Now you and Ricardo are caught in the same deadly game you were watching.

The End

"Let's go back to the house," you say.

"Okay with me."

"Me, too."

Stealthily you creep back down stairs. *Cree-eak!* You almost faint when Lisa steps on the squeaky fourth step. Nothing happens, though. No glowing arrows or disappearing prospectors.

You make it back to the house. Without lighting any lamps, you grab some blankets. You huddle back-to-back in a circle in the middle of the floor, away from the windows. Every noise, imagined or real, makes you jump. The night is long and cold, and it seems endless.

Sunlight on your face wakes you. It's morning! You stand up and stretch. Ricardo and Lisa are still curled up asleep. You wonder why you slept on the parlor floor. Then you remember. The events of last night seem dreamlike—until you glance at the broken window.

You decide to return to the library today; only instead of asking Mrs. Grundy about books to help your search for Great-Uncle Rush's buried fortune, you're going to ask for books on disappearing Indians who shoot disappearing arrows.

The End

"Let's go back to my house."

"Why?" asks Ricardo.

"I think it will be safer. It's too spooky to stay here."

Ricardo and Lisa nod in agreement. You lead the way out the door. You don't feel much like talking, either.

Once on the street, however, you feel even more uneasy than you did in Mr. Phillip's cabin. You feel exposed and vulnerable. Then the silence is broken by your screams as knives appear out of nowhere and bury themselves in your backs.

The End

Out of the corner of your eye you see that Ricardo is motionless, too. The figure comes closer, still flapping and moaning. At the end of the alley it stops. Lisa's voice drifts over to you.

"Scared you, didn't I?"

"Lisa!"

The figure lifts off a sheet to reveal Lisa, almost doubled up with laughter. When she can talk again, she explains.

"You were right about being left alone. I got the creeps the minute you left. I hurried out the door and saw you head down the street. You were walking so cautiously that I decided to scare you. So I rushed inside, grabbed a sheet, and headed over here by the back way." Lisa bursts into laughter again. "Oh, you should have *seen* you two."

Go on to the next page.

"But what are you doing?" she asks when she catches her breath.

"We're going to find out who's moaning."

"The moaning? I thought you went after the red glow."

"We changed our minds."

"Why are you going after the moaning this way?"

"Because Ricardo said he heard it from this direction."

"Well, Ricardo's wrong. It came from the other way. I heard it when I was coming out of the cabin with the sheet."

It's two to one. Should you go back the other way?

If you decide to change direction, turn to page 113.

If you decide to continue as you were, turn to page 84.

"Let's go to the museum. It seems like a safer bet." You stay hidden in the shadows along the way.

The wind has picked up and feels cold on your neck. When you reach the library, you realize the front door is in direct moonlight.

"How are we going to get in?" asks Lisa.

"Oh, shoot. I just realized I left the key that Mrs. Grundy, the librarian, gave me this morning, back at the cabin."

"Is there a back door?" Ricardo asks.

"Yeah, but it's usually bolted."

"We're going to the second floor, right?" asks Lisa.

"Yeah."

"What about the fire escape on the side? Can't we climb up and break a window? I'm sure no one would mind under *these* circumstances."

"Good idea, Lisa!" says Ricardo, and before you can stop him, he is hurrying off. You have no choice but to follow.

Turn to page 103.

"I want to stay in the cabin," you say, but just then Lisa asks, "Do you smell what I smell?"

"Fire!" Ricardo yells. The cabin is ablaze. You look out the window and see a group of Indians and prospectors, weapons at the ready, standing around the cabin.

It looks as if your only choice is the way you will die.

The End

With the tomahawk in your hand, you feel invulnerable. You race fearlessly through the streets.

At the old mining site, you find only Lisa there. "Where's Ricardo?"

"We found something—an old pipe. He went off with it to round up the ghosts. We didn't know if you'd had any luck. Did you find out anything?"

You show Lisa the tomahawk and recite the poem.

"What do we do, though?" she asks. "Will it work to do both?"

"Will Ricardo be able to do it by himself?" You point to the east, where the sky is beginning to lighten. Time is running out.

If you decide to wait for Ricardo, turn to page 110.

If you decide to use the tomahawk, turn to page 97.

"Let's go on," you say, continuing down the ledge before you can change your mind. You glance back: Ricardo and Lisa hesitate, then follow.

When you get to the spot you've picked out, you stop. The place looks perfect. There's a small boulder by the side of the road; you'll be able to hide behind it. You kneel down and feel around for some dirt. You rub a handful on your face.

"What's that for?" Lisa whispers.

"So my face won't be so bright in the moonlight."

You quietly inch into position, take a deep breath to calm yourself, then quickly peek around the boulder. Nothing! You report the absence of any Indians.

"Let me look," says Ricardo, and you change places with him.

"I saw them!" he whispers urgently. "On the cliff. Two people. And maybe some on the road, too."

Turn to page 82.

"Sheriff, we'd like to go back to town with you."

The sheriff is silent for a moment. Then he says, "All right. I guess you'll be safe enough if we stay in your jeep."

The three of you climb into the back of the sheriff's car and head up the road. At the slide, you all transfer to your jeep.

Sam slides behind the wheel and you take off.

Just as you near the cliff where Ricardo says he saw somebody, the sheriff turns to ask you a question. Suddenly the air is filled with bullets and arrows. Sam is the worst hit, and he slumps down, twisting the steering wheel.

The jeep plunges over the cliff and crashes hundreds of feet below. Searchers don't find your bodies for a month.

The End

"Let's try the library. Thinking about going back to the house gives me the creeps."

"You can say that again," says Ricardo.

You remember to warn Lisa and Ricardo about the creaky step, and you silently descend to the street. Hiding in the shadows of buildings, you carefully make your way toward the library.

"Oh, drat!" says Ricardo, the first to spy the library. "The door is in full moonlight."

"Will the key open the back door?" Lisa asks.

"I don't think so," you answer. "Wait—no, it won't. Mrs. Grundy threw the inside bolt on the back door. We have to use the front door."

After a brief pause you say, "Oh, well, the street's clear. I'll unlock the door and slip in. You follow and keep your eyes peeled." You sound braver than you feel. Before you can change your mind, you steal across the street.

You feel strange, standing there in the moonlight, fitting the key into the lock. Your back feels so vulnerable it prickles. You wonder what a knife in the back feels like. The key is stuck! Your breath catches. Then the key turns; the door squeaks a little and opens. You step inside.

"Who's there?" a voice hisses. "I've got a gun."

Turn to page 94.

"Are you sure? I didn't see anyone."

"Yes, I'm sure." Ricardo sounds exasperated. "Look again. I *saw* them."

You're sure you'll see nothing, but when you look again, there they are. Two figures on the cliff and three on the road. Before you can duck, one of the figures turns and looks right at you, or so it seems. Your heart pounds.

"You're right. I think one of them saw me."

"Let's get out of here!" Lisa says.

You want to leave—urgently—but you wonder if you were really seen. Maybe leaving will attract too much attention.

If you decide to leave, turn to page 89.

If you decide to stay put, at least for now, turn to page 116.

"Let's stay here. I know it's spooky, but it's scarier outside."

"I don't think I can go outside," says Lisa.

"It's settled, then," Ricardo says, as he bolts the door.

You'd like to check through Mr. Phillip's library for more information, but you're afraid of ending up dead and gone, too.

The three of you huddle in a corner of the cabin, as far as possible from the spot where Mr. Phillip died. According to the book you read earlier, whatever is happening in High Ridge tonight will end at dawn, but dawn seems a long, long time from now.

The End

"Let's continue this way," you tell the others. "If we don't find anything, we can check out the other end of town."

"Sounds okay to me," Ricardo says.

"Let's go, then!" Lisa is eager to be off, and leads the way.

At Cross Street you turn down to Fifth Street. You remember that there's a small hill at the end of Fifth.

When you reach the end you take the lead and climb to the top of the hill. It is a pile of tailings— the residue left over from an old mine. When you get to the top, you are startled by the figure of a sitting Indian, a blanket wrapped loosely around his shoulders.

As Lisa and Ricardo reach the top the Indian speaks. "Ah, you are all here now. I was wondering where you were. You are late."

Turn to page 98.

"Let's find the chief."

"I see two problems," says Ricardo. "One: we know that the Indian and the prospector ghosts are both dangerous. Two: since we don't know exactly where to find the chief, we might run into the ghosts."

"What should we do?" you ask.

"Well, the best way to find the chief is to split up, which is a dumb idea. As for the ghosts, I think we should disguise ourselves as Indians or prospectors. If we run into them, maybe they won't notice us."

"Ricardo, that's a *stupid* idea," responds Lisa.

You're not so sure.

If you decide to follow Ricardo's idea and disguise yourselves, turn to page 100.

If you agree with Lisa, turn to page 108.

"Let's go."

"Quick! This way," Ricardo says, as he leads you away from the advancing ghosts.

At the edge of the pile of tailings is the abandoned mine shaft building. As you pass the small, brown, weathered building, Ricardo stops and whispers, "Let's hide here and watch."

You're curious to see what the ghosts will do. You wonder if it's dangerous.

If you decide to hide in the building and watch, go on to the next page.

If you decide you'd better keep going, turn to page 109.

You can't resist watching. You slip into the building, Ricardo right behind you, Lisa a reluctant third.

The interior is dark, damp, and cluttered with rusty mining equipment. "Watch out for the open mine shaft," you whisper, as you stumble around it.

There are windows on three sides, grimy with dust and cobwebs. You each look out a window.

"There they are," Lisa whispers, and you and Ricardo quietly move over to her window. You see a ragtag assemblage of Indians and prospectors.

"They look dead," Ricardo whispers.

"They *are* dead," Lisa answers.

"They're not stopping," you say. "They're coming this way!"

"What do we do?"

"It's too late to leave!" Lisa says. "They're almost at the door."

"Quick!" Ricardo says. He pulls himself up the massive beams above the mine shaft, then leans down and helps you and Lisa up. You climb to the highest beam, brushing the cobwebs out of your face and hair.

Turn to page 91.

"Let's go!" Ricardo says. You nod, and the three of you start silently filing back the way you came. Nothing happens, even though it seems as if the world is going to come crashing down on you.

When you get back to the slide you are astounded to find the jeep gone. Lisa discovers a rock with a note on it:

> Have taken jeep.
> County will reimburse expense.
> Sheriff

"What do we do now?" Ricardo wails.

"The sheriff must have gone up to town in our jeep. Let's take his car," you say. "I'm sure it's on the other side of the slide. We can go to Barton City and send a highway crew up to clear the road. Besides I'd just as soon get out of here."

"Same here," says Lisa.

Ricardo looks relieved too, and you are sure you made the right decision when you read in the newspaper the next day about the disappearance of the sheriff—and the other horrors that happened in High Ridge during the night.

The End

Just in time! You are well hidden when the door opens. One ghost follows another inside until no more can fit into the room. Then, with an ear-splitting cry, the first in line jumps into the shaft. One at a time they follow, screaming and moaning horribly.

Lisa holds one hand over her mouth, the other tightly clutching a beam. Ricardo watches carefully, only his eyes moving. You feel shaky, your knees weak.

You watch them all jump into the shaft, wondering if they'll fill the shaft up. Then you realize they're returning to the ground. The last one disappears just as morning sunlight pierces the eastern window. None of you moves for several minutes. Then, stiff-legged, quiet, each absorbed in your own thoughts, you climb down and head out into the clean glare of the sun.

The End

You decide to take the rifle. Lisa and Ricardo gasp when they see it.

"Hey, you look serious."

"I just remembered I'd stuck it back here. It's only a .22, but who knows?" You fling it over your shoulder. "Let's go. There's a place back here that's easy to climb."

You go first because you know the way and can whisper directions to Ricardo and Lisa. Halfway up, you come to the only tricky part of the climb. There's a narrow ledge you have to walk across sideways.

You inch your way across it, then turn to tell Lisa how to get off the ledge. As you turn, the rifle barrel catches on a tree branch jutting out above you. The scraping of the twigs on the metal startles you, and you lose your footing. The branch gives a little shove as it straightens. You fall headlong into the open air.

The sound of you hitting the road is loud in the quiet night. Ricardo and Lisa are on their own now.

The End

Before you can answer the voice in the dark, Ricardo and Lisa push in behind you.

"Close the door! Get out of the way!" they gasp.

"Somebody's here—with a gun," you whisper. Ricardo and Lisa are stunned.

"Close that door and put your hands up," the voice demands.

"Mrs. Grundy? It's me and my friends," you say, closing the door.

"I thought it might be." The voice softens. "I wondered who else would have the key. What are you doing here?"

Go on to the next page.

Swiftly your story tumbles out. When you're done, Mrs. Grundy adds, "It all seems to fit. I heard noises around my house. I didn't see anything and headed next door to Lottie's—Mrs. Howard's house. The door was open. She was sitting in her front parlor, and her face was a mask of horror. She looked dead, but she was only in shock. I laid her on the floor and covered her with a blanket. I tried the phone, but it was dead, like mine. I took her rifle and came here."

"Does the phone work here?" asks Ricardo.

"No. Somebody must have cut the wires."

"Somebody or *something,*" says Lisa.

"Young lady, there are no such things as ghosts. There is a perfectly rational explanation for *everything.*"

"Uh, okay," says Lisa. She doesn't sound convinced, and you aren't either.

"The police will be here soon, I'm sure," says Mrs. Grundy. "I suggest we wait comfortably in the reading room."

There's not much you can do. Mrs. Grundy always gets her way. You settle down for what you are sure will be a long, cold, scary night.

The End

"I can't wait here!" you shout. "C'mon!" And you take off with Lisa away from the direction Ricardo went.

You don't get more than three blocks before you run into a panting Ricardo. "They're right behind me. What do we do now?"

There they are! It looks like hundreds of them. They're running toward you, shouting. Above them you see a curious red glow.

"Watch!" you shout to Ricardo and Lisa. You raise the tomahawk high. At the sight of it, the ghosts stop running; they fall silent.

In clockwise circles above your head, you swing the tomahawk twice.

"Look!" Lisa says in an awed voice. "The ghosts are disappearing!"

Turn to page 104.

"Late?" you ask. "For what?"

"I will try to explain as quickly as possible." He pauses, adjusting his blanket slightly. When he speaks again his voice is grave and formal.

"The prospectors who founded this town long ago left this very spot to the local Indians—my tribe. It was a sacred site to us. Soon after, we performed a burial rite, chanting and waving our ceremonial weapons. The prospectors were drunk. They attacked and killed most of us. There was a reprisal, then a retaliation. My whole tribe was wiped out.

"Later the prospectors came here and dug mine shafts. They kept the gold they found. The bones of my ancestors and the sacred objects they found were discarded in this pile.

"The Spirits in the heavens decided that the ghosts of the murdered—Indians and prospectors alike—must return to this town, where they are compelled to kill each other over and over again—and anyone else unfortunate enough to be caught in the middle."

Go on to the next page.

"How will it end?" Lisa interrupts.

"You will end it. You must dig until you find one of the ceremonial objects the prospectors threw here. Then you must carry it through town. It will protect you. You will use it to gather all the spirits, then return to me. When you have followed these directions the spirits will disappear. They and the town will be at rest.

"Hurry now. All this must be done before dawn or it will be of no use."

You are about to ask questions of the old Indian, but he vanishes before your eyes.

"We'd better hurry," you tell the others. "We don't have much time."

The End

"Ricardo, I'm not sure what there is to your idea, but let's give it a try," you say.

"What do we do about costumes?" Lisa wants to know.

"No problem," you answer. "Back at the cabin there's a trunk filled with all kind of old clothes. I'm sure we can find something to fit."

"Super!" says Ricardo. "C'mon!"

Quickly but cautiously you make your way down the tower stairs and over to your cabin. You find only three costumes that fit, but luckily, they're Indian costumes. You gather in the parlor to decide how to find the chief and conclude that the red glow is the best place to start.

As you leave the cabin, you realize that the costumes aren't as warm as your regular clothes. "It's *cold* outside," says Lisa.

"I guess we have no choice but to act like Indians. Let's go."

Turn to page 102.

"We'd better leave," you say.

"What? Go out there again?" Lisa is aghast.

"Ricardo?"

"Who, me?" Ricardo gulps. "I'll go anywhere or do anything," he says finally, but he doesn't look convincing.

"Let's go, then," you say. "I think we'd better try Ricardo's idea of climbing the church tower and getting a good look around." You move hurriedly out the door, Ricardo behind you. After a pause Lisa follows too.

Turn to page 16.

"I hope this works," murmurs Lisa.

You are put to the test sooner than you hoped. As you turn down the next street, you spy a group of prospector ghosts surrounding the Howard place.

"They've seen us!" Ricardo says. "C'mon, we can't run away now. Try to look as if we're going somewhere." You and Lisa follow him rapidly down the street.

As you get closer to the ghosts, you realize you're shivering. You don't know if it's from cold or fear.

Then you're past them! They glanced at you, but didn't seem to pay much attention. Or so you thought.

You see the ghosts grab both Ricardo and Lisa and feel a knife entering your back. As you fall to the ground, you wonder if it was the shivering that gave you away. Ghosts don't shiver, do they?

The End

As you climb the metal fire escape, you feel very exposed. You have never liked open grating under your feet, and now it feels awful. When you reach the top, Ricardo has already broken the window and crawled in. You start to slide in after him when you hear a shot!

Ricardo groans. You hear a thud as he hits the floor.

Turn to page 105.

She's right. They are gradually fading away. Remembering the next instruction, "as the horror goes," you swing the tomahawk three more times. The ghosts disappear completely.

"Back to the sacred site, quick!" you say, and start running.

When you get there, you find the chief, arms raised to the sky, chanting.

As you approach, he commands, "Give me the tomahawk and the pipe." You and Ricardo obey. The chief smiles. "You have done well," he tells you. "Walk in peace forever and continue to be brave of heart." Then he's gone.

The End

You're not sure what to do: crawl in and see what's happened, or get out of there quickly. It doesn't help to find that you're stuck, and behind you Lisa is urgently whispering: "Hurry up! What happened? Was that a shot? C'mon!"

A woman's voice rings out in the darkness. "Oh, no! I've shot him." It's Mrs. Grundy! As quickly as possible you free yourself and, with Lisa following, rush to Ricardo.

You discover he's just nicked in the shoulder. Lisa gets the first-aid kit and patches him up, while a distraught Mrs. Grundy says that she thought he was a "hooligan" responsible for the "shenanigans" happening that night.

Go on to the next page.

You leave Lisa to console Mrs. Grundy and comfort Ricardo. You find the statue in a glass case. The tomahawk in the chief's hand almost glows with an inner light. The plaque on the case reads:

The following poem was found along with this statue when it mysteriously appeared May 9, 1889, in front of this building. To date no one has determined the meaning of the poem or the origin of the statue.

Swing me twice when the glow arrives,
You'll save yourself and other lives.
Swing me thrice as the horror goes,
You'll bring peace between the foes.

With a whoop, you break the glass, grab the tomahawk from the statue's hands, and leap down the fire escape before a startled Mrs. Grundy or Lisa can stop you.

The End

"Ricardo, I agree with Lisa. Your idea's brilliant, but stupid. C'mon, let's just sneak over to the red glow, the way we sneaked over here."

"Well, *I* like the idea," Ricardo says. He looks annoyed as he turns to descend the stairs. Lisa follows, giving you a grin, and you bring up the rear.

When you reach the bottom of the stairs and step out, Lisa and Ricardo are arguing about which way to go. Lisa says that since you are almost at one end of town it makes sense to investigate it before going back. Ricardo thinks you should follow the original plan and check out the glow.

You decide the only thing to do is toss a coin. It comes up heads.

Turn to page 84.

"Let's get out of here!" you say. Dropping your shovels, you leave quickly, walking away from the approaching ghosts.

You are all silent as you walk hurriedly through the quiet town. When you enter your cabin, you feel safe at home, but you wonder how long it will be until the ghosts return to bring terror back to High Ridge.

The End

"Let's wait here," you say. You sit on the ground, the tomahawk on your lap. You study it; it seems to glow, pulsating gently with a light and power of its own.

"I hope we're making the right decision." Lisa's statement startles you. That's exactly what you were wondering.

The eastern sky keeps brightening. It will be dawn soon—and too late. Just as you are about to tell Lisa you can't wait anymore, she shouts, "Here he comes!"

You can see him now. Ricardo is racing toward you, holding the pipe over his head. Behind him runs a multitude of Indians and prospectors. They are running after Ricardo and shouting loudly.

Ricardo stumbles to a halt in front of you. "Where's the chief?" he pants. "I got the ghosts."

The chief is nowhere in sight. The ghosts keep running. They rush past Ricardo, still shouting.

You wonder where they are going; then you see them pouring into the abandoned mine shaft building. Like a circus act they run into the building until you are sure it can hold no more—and then a few more pile in!

Just as the last ghost disappears, the sun rises.

The End

"Let's go back the other way," you decide. "Is that okay with you, Ricardo?"

"I guess so," Ricardo says. "I mean, it doesn't make any difference to me."

You head up the street. This time you walk in the middle. Somehow with the three of you, everything feels safer. You are sure no harm can come to you.

Suddenly a figure runs toward you shouting, "Run! Run for your lives! They're coming!" You recognize Mr. Burns, the mayor.

"What's going on, Mr. Burns?" you shout.

The answer comes floating back from the now rapidly retreating figure.

"Can't stop. They got the missus. Run for it!"

You shout after him, "*Who* got Mrs. Burns?" but he is too far away. Then you hear something—a thin-sounding and terrifying moaning, and it's coming closer. Whatever got Mrs. Burns is after *you*.

The End

You decide to leave the rifle where it is, so you don't mention it to Lisa.

The path up the cliff is steep, but after about a half hour you finally reach the top. You step up out of the shadows into the yellow moonlight flooding the cliff top.

"Hey, move over," you hear from below. "You're blocking the way."

Ricardo and Lisa step up together and stand next to you.

"Uh-oh," Ricardo says.

Go on to the next page.

Standing in front of you, three old prospectors are shimmering in the moonlight. Each aims a rifle at you.

Your silent questions about what to do are cut short by the bullets.

The End

"Let's stay right here. There's no telling if he really saw me. Besides, we might make more noise leaving."

Lisa and Ricardo agree. You all sit down, wishing you weren't there. Your heart pounds loudly; your limbs feel like lead. You listen intently but hear nothing.

After ten minutes, you take another peek. Still nothing!

"Let's get out of here!" The others can hear the quaver in your voice. You all leave as quickly and quietly as ghosts. You decide you're not coming back here for a long, long time.

The End

ABOUT THE AUTHOR

JULIUS GOODMAN is an editor, designer, and writer of books. He likes reading, sailing, hiking in the mountains, and old Volvos. He lives in north-central Vermont.

ABOUT THE ILLUSTRATOR

PAUL GRANGER is a prize-winning illustrator and painter.

CHOOSE YOUR OWN ADVENTURE

BANTAM
SHOP-AT-HOME
C·A·T·A·L·O·G

Shop at home
for quality childrens books
and save money, too.

Now you can order books for the whole family from
Bantam's latest listing of hundreds of titles including
many fine children's books. *And* this special offer gives
you an opportunity to purchase a Bantam book for
only 50¢. Here's how:

By ordering any five books at the regular price per
order, you can also choose any other single book listed
(up to $4.95 value) for just 50¢. Some restrictions do
apply, so for further details send for Bantam's listing
of titles today.